# Trent and the Fool-Proof Lift

## By

## E. C. Bentley

**British Library Cataloguing-in-Publication Data**
A catalogue record for this book is available from
the British Library

# Contents

# E. C. BENTLEY

Edmund Clerihew Bentley was born in Shepherd's Bush, London in 1875. When he was nineteen, he won a history scholarship to Oxford University, where he became president of the Oxford Union and captain of the university's boat club. After graduating, he studied law in London, and was admitted to the bar in 1902. In this same year, he started working in journalism, the career which would make him famous. Bentley worked primarily at the *Daily News* and the conservative *Daily Telegraph*, but also wrote freelance for a range of publications.

Bentley published a collection of poetry, *Biography for Beginners,* in 1905. His first detective novel, *Trent's Last Case* (1913), was a great critical and commercial success, and many modern critics view it as the first truly modern mystery. Indeed, the *New York Times* dubbed it "one of the few classics of detective fiction." More than twenty years later, he published a sequel, *Trent's Own Case* (1936), and also a book of short stories, *Trent Intervenes* (1938). Between 1936 and 1949, Bentley was president of the Detection Club, contributing to their radio serials.

ONE OF THE commonest forms of fatal accident in the life of the town is falling down a lift shaft. Every coroner of large urban experience has dealt with cases by the score, whether due to short-sight, negligence, faulty construction, or defective safety mechanism. And there is another possibility.

One perfect day in June M. Armand Binet-Gailly, who held an important agency in the wine trade, left his office in Jermyn Street rather earlier than usual, and strolled homewards through the Parks to his bachelor flat at 42 Rigby Street. This was a tall old house, 'converted' from the errors of its pre-Victorian youth. There were five flats, and M. Binet-Gailly's was the second above the ground level. About 5.30 – so went his statement to the police – he entered by the front door which always stood open during the daytime, and went to the lift at the end of the hall. The lift was not at the ground floor, as he could see through the lattice gate, and he pressed the button which should bring it down. But nothing happened.

M. Binet-Gailly was very much annoyed. A portly man, he did not relish the prospect of climbing two flights of stairs on a warm day when he had paid for lift service. He aimlessly seized and shook the handle of the lattice gate. To his amazement, the gate slid aside as if the lift were in place. It should, of course, have been impossible to move it unless the lift were there. The whole system was out of order, he thought. He put his head into the shaft and looked upwards. There was the lift, so far as he could judge, at the top floor. Then, as he drew back his head, his eye was caught by something at the bottom of the shallow well in which the lift-shaft ended. There was a strong electric ceiling lamp always alight at this dark end of the hall, and it showed M. Binet-Gailly quite enough.

Like most of his countrymen, he had served in arms, and things of this kind did not upset him. Plump though he was, he began to clamber down into the well; then he bethought himself. Certainly there could be no life in that crumpled bundle of humanity. The thing to do was to leave it untouched until the arrival of the police. M. Binet-Gailly went to the door communicating with the basement and bellowed downstairs for Pimblett, the caretaker. 42 Rigby Street, though distant by little more than the breadth of Oxford Street from the elegance of Mayfair, did not rise to the luxury of a uniformed porter, and neither Pimblett nor his wife was usually to be seen after the morning job of cleaning the hall and staircase was done.

Pimblett, who also had served in arms, and had seen more dirty work than had M. Binet-Gailly, took in the situation at a glance. Wasting no words, he strode to the hall telephone and rang up the police station. Both men then mounted the stairs to find which gate it was through which the unknown – for the face of the corpse could not be seen – had plunged to his death. On the floor immediately above M. Binet-Gailly's they found the gate drawn back. On this floor was the flat occupied by Mr Anthony Villiers Maxwell – a young man of sporting tastes – and his valet. M. Binet-Gailly proposed ringing the bell of the flat to make inquiries, but Pimblett remarked that the police would prefer to have all that left to them.

An hour later M. Binet-Gailly, sipping a glass of Campari in his own rooms, discussed with his servant, by name Aristide, what he had just learnt of this mysterious affair. The dead man had turned out to be his own landlord, Mr Stephen Havelock Hermon, who had bought the house a few years before, and had installed his nephew, Anthony Maxwell, in the flat above-stairs on its falling vacant soon afterwards. There had been some slight lack of sympathy between M. Binet-Gailly and Mr Hermon, owing to the fact that Mr Hermon had among his eccentricities a passionate hatred of liquor in every form, and when he purchased the place had not concealed his chagrin on finding that one of the sitting tenants was engaged in the wine trade, which Mr Hermon preferred to call the drink-traffic.

No one in the building had seen Mr Hermon enter it that afternoon. No one had seen him at all before the finding of his body. No one had known of his intention to come to the house. Mr Clayton Haggett, the famous surgeon, who had the top flat, had not been at home; his housekeeper had heard no ring. Anthony Maxwell also had been out, and his valet had had the afternoon 'off'. Aristide could vouch for it, as he had already informed the police that no one had called at M. Binet-Gailly's. Mr Lucian Corderoy, the eminent dress designer, and his wife had both been at his shop in Malyon Street, and their 'daily' servant was never in the place after twelve noon. As for Sir George Stower, the Keeper of Phoenician Antiquities at the British Museum, he was enjoying a hard-earned holiday at Margate, and his flat on the ground floor had been shut up for some days past.

'But naturally,' remarked Aristide, fingering a swarthy chin, 'the old gentleman wished to call upon his nephew.'

'It is very probable,' M. Binet-Gailly agreed. 'He was devoted to that young animal, and they say he had no other relative living. The nephew will be his heir, no doubt, and he will make the money roll a little faster than the uncle ever did.'

'Ah! when one is young,' observed Aristide sentimentally.

'And when one is a waster by nature,' M. Binet-Gailly added. 'Well, Aristide, it is time for me to dress.'

Philip Trent, in his first outline of the case for the readers of the *Record*, had given these facts about the other tenants of the building. 'It is naturally assumed [he wrote] that Mr Hermon had called, as he often did, to see his nephew, to whom he is said to have been much attached. His ringing at the door had been resultless, and he had turned away to go down by the way he had come. He had opened the gate, believing the lift to be in position there – and stepped out into emptiness. He was known to be extremely short-sighted. His neck, so says the police surgeon, was broken, and there were other injuries that must have been immediately fatal. When his body was found he had been dead not more than an hour.

'This is very simple, but it leaves all the important questions unanswered.

'Why was not the lift where he expected it to be? He had only just left it; and according to the information gathered by the police there had been no one leaving or entering any of the flats since the early afternoon, when Mr Clayton Haggett and Mr Maxwell went out.

'Why was it at the top floor?

'How was it that he had been able to open the gate, which should have been locked automatically the moment the lift moved from that floor?

'Why was the gate on the ground floor unlocked? Why

indeed? Conceivably the mechanism of the upstairs gate had gone wrong, so that Mr Hermon could open it; but the gate at the bottom could not be opened by a dead man.

'Why were all the other gates in working order – the top gate, where the lift was, unlocked; the other two locked?

'On this very vital point I have had some conversation with the expert who was sent to investigate by the firm which built and installed the lift. The mechanism, he told me, was tested by the makers at monthly intervals, and had been in perfect order at the last examination, ten days before. The system was as nearly fool-proof as it could be. "But," he added, "it isn't tool-proof. Any engineer could see with half an eye that both those locks had been forced."

'Here are the elements of a very sinister mystery. Some one who was not Mr Hermon forced the ground-floor gate. Presumably he forced the other. The only persons known to have been in the house from three o'clock onwards were the caretaker in the basement, the French manservant in M. Binet-Gailly's flat, and the housekeeper in Mr Haggett's. Did some one enter the house before Mr Hermon; or did some one accompany him? To this point the inquiries of the police are being directed – so far, I believe, without result.

'If Mr Hermon was a victim of violence, it is hard to think that any feeling of ill-will could have been at work. It is true that he was a man of strong opinions, often violently expressed in public controversy – the hard knocks exchanged between him and his tenant, Mr Clayton Haggett, in their dispute over vivisection last year will be remembered. But he was always a fair and even a chivalrous fighter, on the friendliest footing with opponents to whom he was personally known. His nature was kindly and generous, his great wealth was largely devoted to works of benevolence; the hospital endowments made by him as memorials to his late wife are but a part of his service to humanity.'

Trent did not try to intrude on the sorrow of Anthony Maxwell, but he had from the young man's valet, Joseph Weaver, some material information. He learnt that the nephew felt his loss very deeply indeed; that he did not look like the same man. He had, Weaver said, a feeling heart. A little wild he might have been – young gentlemen would be young gentlemen – but he had what they call a nice nature. He owed everything to Mr Hermon, who had been a father to him after his parents died when he was a child. Naturally he was very much upset.

Trent reflected privately on the deceitfulness of appearances; for he knew Anthony Maxwell by sight, and would not have said that either his eye, his mouth, or his bearing proclaimed the niceness of his nature. Perhaps Weaver was being loyal to his employer. He did not look particularly loyal; but then he did not look anything to speak of. He had the expressionlessness of his calling. His quiet voice, neat clothes, and sleek black hair suggested nothing but discretion. Trent asked a question.

Mr Hermon, Weaver said, came up fairly often on business from his place in Surrey, and when he did so, always visited his nephew. Sometimes he came on purpose to see him. No; Mr Maxwell had not been expecting him on the day of the accident; he had given no notice that he was coming. If he had done so, Mr Maxwell would naturally have been at home. Weaver thought it unlikely that Mr Hermon had been intending to call on any of the other tenants. He did do so from time to time, to talk about some matters of repairs or other landlord's business; but that would always be by appointment, and not during the working day. All the tenants, Weaver pointed out, were busy men, with the exception of Mr Maxwell; they would seldom be at home until the evening.

Yes; Mr Hermon attended personally to the management of all his house property in the West End. There was a good deal of it, and it gave him occupation. No; he was not what they call a hard landlord; quite the contrary, Weaver would say. Mr Hermon liked to do things for people, being a very generous man, as Weaver had good reason to know.

'You mean that he was generous to you,' Trent suggested. 'A present for you when he called here – that sort of thing?'

'Mr Hermon always behaved like a gentleman,' Weaver said demurely. 'But I meant more than that, sir. You see, I was two years in his service before I came to Mr Maxwell; that is how I came to know so much about his habits, and to appre- ciate his kindness. Then when Mr Hermon went on a tour round the world, he suggested I should go to Mr Maxwell, who was not satisfied with the valet he had then; and I have remained in his service since then – about nine months ago it would be.'

When Trent went to talk it over with his friend Chief-Inspector Bligh, he found that officer cheerfully interested in what he described as a very nice case.

'There's nothing easy,' he said, 'about it so far. Of course, it's a murder – that's certain. You have heard what the lift company's man says. And, of course, it was meant to look as if it might be an accident.'

'Then how about the ground-floor gate being forced as well as the other? That doesn't look like an accident.'

'Well, what does it look like?' Mr Bligh wanted to know.

'It looks to me as it looks to you, I suppose. When the old man had been pushed into the lift-shaft, the murderer realized that something had gone wrong with his plan. Hermon had had something on him that might give the murderer away if it was found on the body. The only thing for him to do was to run downstairs, prise open the bottom gate, and take what he wanted off the body. If Pimblett or anybody appeared while he was doing so, he could say he had seen the old man open the gate and fall down the shaft, and had rushed down and forced the gate to see if he was still alive.'

The inspector nodded. 'Yes; that's the idea. And he did get what he wanted, presumably; and nobody did see him. Of course, it's the sort of place where nobody is about most of the time, and the man who did the job knew that.'

'Well, how about the people who live here? Are they all above suspicion?'

'There is no such thing,' Mr Bligh declared, 'as being above suspicion – not if I do the suspecting. And it just happens that most of them haven't an alibi. The Museum man has, of course; his flat was shut up, and is still. And the Corderoys were at their dress shop till after six. But the Frenchman was alone when he came in and reported having found the body; and his story of how he found it, and what time he entered the house, is quite unsupported. Maxwell says he lunched at his flat, went out immediately afterwards, and spent all the afternoon at Lord's watching Lancashire take a licking from Middlesex; then went to his club with some other bright boys, had drinks, and came home to dress for dinner. But Lord's is a place you can dodge out of and return to later, and it's no distance for a car to Rigby Street. Then there's Clayton Haggett, the surgeon. He had lunch in his flat too, after a morning at the hospital; went down to his car at two-thirty, had an operation at a nursing-home and another at a private house; finished by four-fifteen, had a cup of tea, and then spent two hours driving about down Richmond way – just to take the air, and nobody with him all that time, which is a pity.'

'He didn't like Hermon,' Trent remarked. 'He was very bitter in that tussle they had over vivisection.'

'Yes, and he's got a naughty temper when he's crossed. Loses his self-control. He had to resign from the Hunter Club for knocking a man down in the smoking-room. Nobody would have anything to do with him if he wasn't such a wizard with the knife.'

'And what about the servants in the building? Do they come into the picture at all?'

'All I can tell you is that none of their stories can be checked. Pimblett says he was in the basement all the afternoon until the Frenchman shouted for him; his wife was away calling on her sister in Highbury. The French manservant and Haggett's housekeeper say they never opened the doors of their flats until the police looked them up after the finding of the body. Maxwell's man says he had the afternoon off, went out after his master had gone, and sat through the cinema programme at the Byzantine, getting back a little before Anthony did. Well, what good's that? Like the other three, he can't prove anything at all about where he was for some hours before the police were called in.'

'Any of them ever been in trouble?'

'Nothing known against any of them. Ex-Sergeant Pimblett – excellent record. Mrs Hargreaves, the housekeeper – ditto. Weaver used to be employed at Harding's the big barber shop in Duke Street, where old Hermon used to go when he was in town. He always had Weaver to attend to him, and, at last he took him on as his valet. Afterwards—'

'Yes, he told me; he was switched on to Anthony. Perfectly respectable. And the French domestic?'

'All I know about Aristide Recot is that he has a wooden face and side-whiskers, and doesn't mind being seen in an apron. What I'm told by his master is that he has been with him for some years, and given every satisfaction. But what's the use? We had to consider the servants, of course; but what motive could any of them have had? It's a different thing when you come to their employers. Haggett, for instance.'

Trent looked the inspector in the eyes. 'You were talking about motive,' he said gently. 'Is Haggett's resentment really the strongest you can think of? I don't like being teased.'

'All right; I was coming to it,' Mr Bligh responded with a faint grin. 'Yes, I suppose the expectation of coming into the greater part of a very large fortune might operate as a motive. That is what Maxwell will do, according to our information. Unless something happens to him. His uncle made him a very generous allowance, and he lived rent free, and Weaver's wages were paid by the old man. Maxwell ought to have been grateful, and perhaps he was; but there you are – he's a vicious young brute, and always in debt; and though Hermon wasn't strong, he might have lived to any old age. Now then! Will that do for you?'

'Something of the sort had crossed my mind,' Trent admitted. 'Certainly it will do – until something better comes along.'

Mr Bligh raised an impressive finger. 'And now,' he said, 'I'll tell you something that hadn't crossed your mind. It's information received. If it's right, the coroner will hear it at a later stage, but at present we would rather the murderer didn't know about it. You remember I mentioned that Clayton Haggett left his flat at two-thirty that afternoon. Well, he had more to tell us than that. He went down by the lift, he said. It's rather a slow-motion lift. As it passed down by the floor below – Anthony's floor – Haggett heard some words spoken. He could see as he passed that the door of the flat was just being opened from inside, and as it opened he heard a loud bullying voice call out, ' You do what I say, and look sharp about it. If you get on the wrong side of me, you know what to expect.' That is as near as Haggett can go to the actual words he heard – I asked him to be particular.'

Trent stared at the inspector with kindling eyes. 'You do like saving up the best bit to the last, don't you? And you had this – this! – simply handed to you. On a plate.'

'With parsley round it,' added Mr Bligh unashamed.

'I have heard you use that phrase before,' Trent said thoughtfully. 'It meant, I think, that you were rather mistrustful of good things that came so easily. But now, what about this remarkable addition to the record? Did Haggett recognize the voice? Did he see anybody?'

'No. Haggett says it might have been Maxwell he heard talking; but he only knows Maxwell by sight, has never spoken to him, and has no idea what his voice would sound like if it was raised. And, of course, it might have been anybody else in the world. Then I asked him what class of voice it was – like a curate's, or a dustman's, or what. All he could tell me was that it was not a coarse voice, and not a refined one; just middling. Very useful! But that isn't all. As the lift got to the bottom he heard a door above slam violently, which he assumed to be the one he had just seen being opened; and as he was getting into his car, Maxwell came out of the street door, with his hat on, looking furiously angry and very red in the face, and walked away rapidly.

Trent considered this. 'So that is Haggett's information. And what does Maxwell say about it?'

'He hasn't been asked – yet. He is being given a little more time to make mistakes. But, of course, it may all be a lie. Yes, you may look surprised; but Haggett isn't out of it yet, as I told you. There's another piece of news I've got for you which certainly isn't a lie. When Jackson did the post mortem he found something that wants a lot of explaining.'

'What! Another thing you are keeping dark?'

'For the present. He noticed that the finger nails of the right hand looked as if they had been scratching hard at something, and there was a very faint odour that he couldn't place; so he took some scrapings from the nails to be analyzed. They found some tiny scraps of human skin; also traces of some things with hydrocarbo scientific names that don't seem to tell you much, and one thing that I have heard of quite often before.'

'Yes. What?'

'Chloroform.'

Thinking it over in his studio, Trent could make no more of this at first than Mr Bligh and he had made between them. If there had been a struggle, and if chloroform had been used, it did seem to point to the one resident in the house who might be presumed to know all about chloroform and what could be done with it. And Haggett was known to be violent tempered and a good hater, as well as a very able and successful professional man – not an unknown combination of qualities. But Trent found it hard to believe in such a character expressing its dislike in murder done by tricky and treacherous means. A quarrel; yes. An assault; possibly. An assault with a fatal result, legally a murder; such things did happen. But a planned and cold-blooded crime, with the murderer scheming to avoid detection by means of a trumped-up tale – Trent did not see it. In his experience, trained faculties, high responsibility, and professional distinction did not go with dirty actions and circumstantial lying.

But if Haggett's story of what he had heard and seen was true, how could it be fitted to the known facts? Maxwell's own statement about the time at which he had left the building agreed with Haggett's. Weaver's statement was that he had, as was natural, gone out a little later. Both of them had said nothing of this loud-voiced unknown who had used threatening language in Maxwell's flat. It might have been Maxwell himself. Could it have been Hermon? But Hermon had been fond, even foolishly fond, of his nephew. Unless – and here opened a new vista of ugliness – both Maxwell and his servant had been concealing the truth on that point, building up the fiction of a generous benefactor whom for worlds Maxwell would not have injured. There might be purpose enough in their doing so. The inspector had not thought of that; at least (Trent reflected with a wry smile) he had not mentioned it. Hermon's visit, by the way, had been a surprise visit according to Weaver.

Trent, at this point in his meditations, rose and began to pace the studio. Soon he went across to the model's dressing-room and examined his appearance in the mirror there. His hair had been cut fairly recently, but another trimming would not upset the balance of nature, he thought. Within the hour he was one of a dozen sheeted forms, sitting in a strange chair before a tall mirror, and had met the attendant's opening comment on the warmth of the day with the due rejoinder that it looked like rain later on.

Trent, like many other men, found his thoughts the clearer for being written down, and would often prepare for the drafting of a dispatch that could be published by a private memorandum, including all that could not. That evening he sat at his bureau, and did not rise until the account of what he had discovered, and the conclusions drawn, was complete in black and white.

'Starting with the belief that Haggett's story was true [he wrote], I had to make out who the person in Maxwell's flat was who gave some order, in offensive words, coupled with a vague threat; and who the person ordered about and threatened was. As Bligh said, it might have been any one who used those words; some one who had not as yet come into view in the case. But it was as well to consider first those who were known to have been in the place; and one of these was Hermon. But the accounts we had of Hermon made this seem unlikely; and they were not only the accounts given by Maxwell and his valet. Hermon's general reputation was that of a man who would be the last in the world to bully and threaten. As for the others who had been in the other flats, there was no visible shadow of a reason for suspecting any one of them.

'There remained Maxwell and his valet.

'Maxwell might be capable of bullying and threatening. He is not a nice young man. Could he have been the speaker, and either Hermon or Weaver the man spoken to?

'Well, is it likely? Maxwell is not a lunatic. No man in his senses would talk like that to his rich uncle whose fortune he expected to inherit; nor to his valet unless he was prepared for the man leaving him on the spot, and for being obliged to do his own valeting and cooking and housework until he could get another servant. Unless, of course, he had got either of them under his thumb in some way. Has Hermon, or Weaver, a guilty past, known to Maxwell?

'I had got as far as this when a new point occurred to me. Weaver, when I saw him, had told me that Maxwell had not been expecting his uncle's visit. As this looked very much like a plain lie, I thought some attention paid to Weaver might be worth the trouble; and so I went and had my hair cut at Harding's.

'The man who cut it was as ready for conversation as barbers usually are. I spoke of the fatal accident to Mr Hermon, and the barber, who may have been reading my own remarks on the subject, said that it was a funny sort of accident, giving his reasons for that view. Then I mentioned that I knew Mr Hermon's former valet had once had a job at Harding's. The man remembered both of them very well. He only wished he had the chance of bettering himself as Weaver had done. He had not known that Weaver had become Mr Maxwell's valet, but he had known that Weaver had done very well for himself. Besides that, Weaver had come into a bit of money of his own; he had mentioned it confidential. He was quite the gentleman now, especially in the last six months. He had taken to having his hair done at Harding's once a fortnight, probably just to show off a bit among his old pals. Gold wrist-watch, diamond tie-pin, quite the swell. Liked to do himself well, too, in his time off; and why not if you could run to it? Sometimes he would have my barber and other friends from Harding's to meet him after hours, and would stand drinks like a lord; and you could always see he had had a few beforehand.

'So far, my visit to Harding's had yielded more than I had any right to expect. But this was not all. My man came at length to that stage of the proceedings at which it is usual for the barber to hint delicately that the condition of one's scalp is not all that could be wished, and that this could be remedied by the use of some sort of hair-wash. With a flash of inspiration I asked what Weaver was in the habit of buying for himself. The best hair tonic there is, said my barber with enthusiasm; Harding's own preparation, Capillax – just the thing for me; and I would understand that Weaver knew, as a hairdresser, how excellent it was. I thought, when I was told the price of it, that Weaver also knew how impressively costly it was. I was shown a bottle of Capillax; a green fluted bottle, with NOT TO BE TAKEN stamped in the glass. Why, I asked my barber, should I be forbidden to take Capillax if I should choose to buy Capillax?

'He turned the bottle over, and showed me on the back a tiny pasted label. It read:

This preparation, containing among other valuable
ingredients a small amount of Chloroform, is, in
accordance with the Pharmacy Act, hereby labelled
POISON.

'I ordered a bottle, of course. I thought my barber had earned his commission on the sale. And I asked him if he could tell me why chloroform should be used in a tonic for the hair, because I had thought it was for putting people to sleep. He said yes, but that was only the vapour of chloroform; in solution it acted as a stimulant to the skin, and had cleansing properties.

'My reconstruction of this crime is that Weaver planned the murder of Hermon. He had found out something that Maxwell did not dare have known about himself; he put the screw on him and bled him for every shilling he could raise. A servant who knows too much about his employer is a figure common enough in the odorous annals of blackmail. Weaver had 'come into money' indeed! Probably he got rid of a lot of it by betting. Anyhow, the more he got, the more he wanted. He had tasted easy money; he could not do without it; and there was no more in sight. But he knew that Maxwell, when his uncle died, would be a rich man. Weaver thought it over; and he formed a plan, to be carried out the first time that opportunity offered.

'On the morning of Hermon's death Maxwell heard, by letter or telephone, that his uncle intended to call that afternoon. Weaver's tale, that the old man had given no notice of his coming, was hardly credible. It was the height of summer, and it was utterly unlikely that Maxwell would be staying indoors that afternoon unless he was expecting a visitor. Hermon would certainly have let him know he was coming. This was what Weaver had been waiting for. After lunch he told Maxwell to leave the flat, go somewhere where he could mix with friends, and stay away until dinner-time. I do not believe Maxwell knew what was intended, because Haggett's story makes it plain that he protested against this. He did not see why he should deliberately absent himself when his uncle had asked him to be at home; why should he affront the old man? Weaver then went to the door of the flat, and as he opened it he raised his voice in the bullying words that Haggett caught as the lift went down. Maxwell, in a furious temper, did as he was told.

'When Hermon arrived, coming up by the lift, Weaver

opened the door to him. He framed some lie to account for Maxwell's absence, and asked him to come in, perhaps for a rest and a cup of tea. Hermon did so; and while he was alone in the sitting-room, Weaver slipped out, took the lift to the floor above, and forced the lift gate on Maxwell's floor. When the old man went, Weaver saw him to the lift, opened the gate, and thrust him into the empty shaft. He knew better than most people how bad Hermon's sight was, and how little strength he had for a struggle. And here the plan went wrong. Hermon realized at the last instant that the lift was not there, and grabbed at Weaver as he felt the push given him. His right hand clutched Weaver's hair, tearing some of it out as he fell to his death, and lacerating the man's scalp.

'Weaver had seen instantly that if hair was found in the dead man's hand there would be an end of the theory that he had met with an accident. The police would be looking for a man with black hair and a scratched head; and they would not have far to look. There was only one thing for it. Weaver ran down to the ground floor, forced the gate there, stepped into the well, and carefully removed the hair he found in the dead man's grasp. There was nothing else he could do. He must simply stick to the story he had already made up, and trust to luck. After all, as far as he knew, there had been no witness whatever to anything that had passed.'

It was late by the time Trent had finished his memorandum. He read and re-read it, then slipped it into an envelope, addressed it to Mr Bligh at Scotland Yard, went out and registered it at the district post office.

Trent was at work in his studio next morning when the telephone bell called him.

Mr Bligh, not an effusive man by nature, said that Trent's report had reached him. 'There's no doubt but what you're right,' he went on. 'It's a pity, though, that we shall never hear what it was Weaver knew about Maxwell. It might very well have been a job for us.'

'Well, you called him a vicious young brute,' Trent said. 'With my morbid imagination and your fund of horrid experience, we ought to be able to guess a few of the things that it might have been. But why do you say you will never know? If you bring the murder home to Weaver, he will probably give Maxwell away, having no further use for his secret. It would be just like him.'

'Weaver won't do that.' There was a note of grimness in the inspector's voice. 'At eight fifteen last night Weaver was on his way down Coventry Street. He had been drinking, and couldn't walk straight. A dozen people saw him stumble off the kerb and into the road, right under a passing bus. He was killed instantly. His injuries—'

'Thanks, I don't want to hear about his injuries.' Trent wiped his brow. 'They were fatal – that's enough for me.'

'Yes, but there were some that weren't fatal. On the head, concealed by the hair, there were four deep scratches, not completely healed, and the signs of some hair having been torn out by the roots. I thought you'd like to know.'

www.ingramcontent.com/pod-product-compliance
Lightning Source LLC
Chambersburg PA
CBHW030532260626
47157CB00005B/2002